Don't miss any of the titles
in the ALIEN INVADERS series:

www.randomhousechil...

D0183720

ALIEN INVADERS: TANKA, THE BALLISTIC BLASTER
A RED FOX BOOK 978 1 849 41239 1

First published in Great Britain by Red Fox,
an imprint of Random House Children's Publishers UK
A Random House Group Company

This edition published 2012

1 3 5 7 9 10 8 6 4 2

Text and illustrations copyright © David Sinden,
Guy Macdonald and Matthew Morgan, 2012
Cover and interior illustrations, map and gaming cards by Dynamo Design
Designed by Nikalas Catlow

The right of David Sinden, Guy Macdonald and Matthew Morgan
to be identified as the authors of this work has been asserted in accordance
with the Copyright, Designs and Patents Act 1988.

The Random House Group Limited supports the Forest Stewardship
Council® (FSC®), the leading international forest certification organisation.
Our books carrying the FSC label are printed on FSC® certified paper.
FSC is the only forest certification scheme endorsed by the leading
environmental organisations, including Greepeace.
Our paper procurement policy can be found at
www.randomhouse.co.uk/environment

MIX
Paper from
responsible sources
FSC
www.fsc.org   FSC® C016897

Set in Century Schoolbook

Red Fox Books are published by
Random House Children's Publishers UK,
61–63 Uxbridge Road, London W5 5SA

www.randomhousechildrens.co.uk
www.randomhouse.co.uk

Addresses for companies within The Random House Group Limited can be
found at: www.randomhouse.co.uk/offices.htm

THE RANDOM HOUSE GROUP Limited Reg. No. 954009

A CIP catalogue record for this book is available from
the British Library.

Printed and bound in Great Britain by CPI Group, (UK) Ltd,
Croydon, CR0 4YY

ALIEN INVADERS

MAX SILVER

TANKA
THE BALLISTIC BLASTER

RED FOX

THE GALAXY

Cosmo's route ----

DELTA QUADRANT

GAMMA QUADRANT

STARFLIGHT SPACESHIP
MANUFACTURING COMPANY

PLANET SYN-NOVA

PLANET BALAZ

SYSTEM OPEX

ALPHA QUADRANT

MOON OF GARR

GALACTIC CORE

BETA QUADRANT

THE WRECKING ZONE

PLANET KEFU

RESISTANCE IS FUTILE, EARTHLINGS!

MY NAME IS KAOS, AND MY WAR WITH YOUR GALAXY IS ENTERING A NEW PHASE...

THE YEAR IS 2121 AND I HAVE JOINED FORCES WITH METALLICON ALIENS FROM THE UNIVERSE'S WRECKING ZONE. THEY HAVE THE POWER OF LIVING MACHINES, AND I AM PROGRAMMING THEM TO INVADE YOUR GALAXY.

YOUR SECURITY FORCE, G-WATCH, WILL BE POWERLESS TO DEFEND YOU, AND ITS EARTHLING AGENT, COSMO SANTOS, WILL BE ANNIHILATED ALONG WITH HIS FRIENDS.

RESISTANCE IS FUTILE, EARTHLINGS. THE GALAXY WILL BE MINE!

INVADER ALERT!

In the cargo hold of an interstellar livestock transporter, Ranger Cron kept watch over a waking meglaphant: a mighty mammoth-like beast being transported from the thawing ice-planet Slok to the galactic Life Sanctuary on Planet Kefu. The beast seemed agitated after its journey, and swung its long trunk against the wall of the hold.

"There, there. You're nearly at your

new home," Ranger Cron said, stroking the beast's white fur with his scaly Kefuan hand.

He reached for one of its tusks to steady himself as the ship landed with a jolt. The engines died down and, at the back of the hold, hydraulic bolts were released, while a large exit ramp extended downwards. Bright daylight flooded in and Ranger Cron led the meglaphant out onto the straw-covered landing area of a warm, forested planet. The beast trumpeted contentedly.

"Happy to have arrived, eh?" Ranger Cron said to it. "You'll like it here, I promise. This is just the start of things."

More transporter ships were landing nearby. Life Sanctuary rangers led other alien creatures down their ramps: emerald-and-black zebraves from the shrinking Planet Bol; giant meteor slugs from storma-space; a herd of walrakk from the polluted seas of Organa, and even hairy ape-flowers and giant walking goak trees. All were being taken across the landing area to large stone pyramids among the trees.

Ranger Cron guided the meglaphant towards a vast footbath of disinfectant where a ranger was checking the creatures in. "An adult male meglaphant for sanctuary dimension C19," Ranger Cron called.

More rangers were hosing the creatures down, ensuring that no infectious diseases were brought into the wildlife sanctuary from across the galaxy.

But just as Ranger Cron reached the disinfection area, the meglaphant came to a stop. "Come on, it's only the footbath," the ranger said, gently tugging the beast's fur to encourage it on.

The other creatures began behaving oddly too: birds screeched, zebraves bolted and walrakk bellowed, all clearly agitated. Amidst their noise the meglaphant raised its trunk to the sky, trumpeting a terrified "Harrrooo!"

Ranger Cron looked up and saw a large object coming down through Kefu's atmosphere, heading directly for the landing area. *What is that thing?* he wondered anxiously. It wasn't a spaceship; it was coming in too fast.

It crashed down, obliterating a transporter ship and gouging a crater in the ground.

Beasts fled into the trees, and the terrified meglaphant reared up, almost trampling Ranger Cron. A huge machine-like alien trundled out of the crater, rolling on caterpillar tracks like a tank. It had rusty-red armour plating and an arm like a cannon. It fired a neutron blast at one of the pyramids, blowing it to pieces; its second blast destroyed another transporter ship and sent shrapnel flying. A piece struck the meglaphant and it trumpeted with pain. "*Harrrroooo!*"

The alien swung its cannon arm, preparing to fire again. "I am Tanka, and I'm here to blow this place up!"

CHAPTER ONE

THE LIFE SANCTUARY

Cosmo piloted the Dragster 7000 spaceship along Hyperway 10 between the Alpha and Beta quadrants of the galaxy. He had his helmet off, and Brain-E, the ship's bug-like brainbot, was attaching sensors to either side of his head.

"It's called the snack-o-matic, Master Cosmo," Brain-E said. "It's the latest in in-flight snack technology. All you have to do is picture a snack in your mind." Wires led from the sensors to a see-through hatch at the front of the control desk.

"OK, I'm picturing it," Cosmo replied, thinking about a Buzz Bar, his favourite chocolate bar from back on Earth. He imagined its golden wrapper, the taste of chocolate and sticky peanut butter on his tongue . . . He heard a hum from the hatch in the control desk, and looked down to see something materializing inside. With a clang, the hatch sprang open, and he reached his hand in and retrieved it. It was a Buzz Bar, a real one! Cosmo grinned. "I could use a

snack-o-matic back home on Earth. It would save me a fortune in pocket money!"

Brain-E swivelled its bug eyes. "It should give you an energy boost for the battle ahead."

Cosmo was on the final stage of a mission for the galactic security force G-Watch: to defeat five alien invaders – metallicons from the Wrecking Zone being beamed into the galaxy under the command of the outlaw Kaos. Cosmo had so far defeated four of them: Krush, the iron giant, Junkjet, the flying menace, Minox, the planet driller, and Zipzap, the rebel racer. Now he was flying to Planet Kefu, home of the galactic Life Sanctuary, to face the fifth and final invader: Tanka.

Cosmo ate a chunk of Buzz Bar, and as he flew through the galaxy its taste brought back memories of his old life on Earth: his mum, his home, his friends. He offered a piece to his Etrusian co-pilot,

Agent Nuri. "Nuri, try this. It's the most delicious chocolate bar ever."

Nuri was busy checking the spaceship's navigation console. "Thanks, Cosmo," she replied, popping the piece in her mouth. "Now get ready to exit hyperdrive."

Cosmo gripped the controls, looking out at the flashing beacons of Hyperway 10. He flicked a silver switch on the steering column and felt his ears pop as the Dragster exited hyperdrive. The craft slowed to eleven vectrons, and stars reappeared in the spacescreen. Cosmo tapped the screen, activating the star plotter, and words flashed up naming the objects in view:

PLANET VISTO . . . PLANET FEX . . . PLANET KEFU . . .

"Here we go," he said, steering the Dragster towards the small green planet labelled Kefu. He summoned his courage, preparing to face his next opponent, and his spacesuit began to glow. He was wearing

the Quantum Mutation Suit, body armour that allowed him to mutate into alien forms. It was activated by the power of the universe – a power present in all living things but uniquely strong in Cosmo.

As the Dragster flew through Planet Kefu's atmosphere, Cosmo looked down, seeing trees below. "Is this whole place a wildlife reserve?" he asked.

"The galactic Life Sanctuary on Planet Kefu is a multi-dimensional reserve for endangered species, Master Cosmo, with many different habitats that exist far beyond what you can see below," Brain-E replied.

"Multi-dimensional?" Cosmo asked, curious.

"That's right. Each dimension is accessed via pyramid portals built by the Kefuan rangers."

Cosmo had heard about portals in Space Studies back at school on Earth; they were access routes into other dimensions of space-time. But he'd never dreamed he would ever get to see any.

"G-Watch scanners report that Tanka struck west of here," Nuri said. "Near the Life Sanctuary's main landing area."

Cosmo flew west, looking out for signs of the invader. "OK, Brain-E, what do we know about this alien?"

"According to G-Watch reconnaissance probes, Tanka is a metallicon evolved from discarded military hardware. He is armed with a ballistic neutron blaster and is capable of massive destruction."

As the Dragster flew above more trees, Cosmo saw a landing area cut into a swathe of forest where smoke was rising from destroyed transporter ships. A crater had been gouged in the ground, and nearby, several ancient-looking stone pyramids had been blasted, some reduced to rubble.

"It looks like Tanka's blown the place to pieces," Nuri said.

Cosmo watched Kefuan rangers chasing after alien beasts: striped zebraves, black blubbery walrakks and even hairy ape-like plants. He circled, looking for Tanka, but could see no sign of the invader. "OK, team, I'm taking us in to land," he said.

As the spaceship touched down, he flicked a switch, opening the exit door.

Cosmo stepped down onto the landing
area, and Nuri and Brain-E followed. It
was mayhem outside. Huge transporter
ships were on fire, startled creatures
were running loose, and patrol buggies,
jetbikes and trailers had been destroyed
or overturned.

Cosmo led the way past a herd of
antogs and ducked as a fork-tailed drocox
flew overhead. He splashed through a
trough of disinfectant and saw a white-
furred mammoth-like beast lying injured
on the ground, a Kefuan ranger at its side.
"What happened here?" Cosmo asked him.

The ranger looked startled to see them, his scales a pale green colour.

"We're from G-Watch," Nuri said reassuringly. "We're here to help."

"A machine-like alien beamed down and started firing at us," the Kefuan explained. "I'm Ranger Cron, and this is a rare meglaphant, one of only seven left

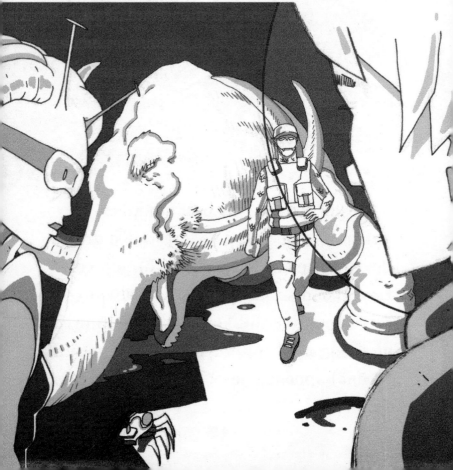

in the galaxy. It's dying." The creature had a large piece of shrapnel in its side and was losing blood. Its tongue had flopped out and it was panting. "The medical bay was destroyed in the attack," Ranger Cron continued. "I don't know what to do."

Cosmo looked into the meglaphant's enormous bloodshot eyes. "We'll save you," he said to it.

"I'm afraid it could be too late for that," Ranger Cron replied. "Its wounds are too large to stitch."

Nuri was looking around for Tanka, her phaser gun at the ready. "Cosmo, we must locate the invader," she said urgently.

"You find out where it went, Nuri, while I try to fix this beast," Cosmo replied. He took hold of the meglaphant's thick white fur and pulled himself up its front leg to the chunk of shrapnel in its side. "I've got an idea how we might save it."

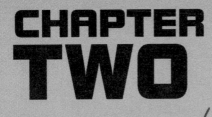

CHAPTER
TWO

OPERATION MEGLAPHANT

While Nuri searched for Tanka, Cosmo
took hold of the huge chunk of metal
poking out of the meglaphant's side. It was
a twisted panel from a transporter, and
was deeply embedded. He carefully heaved
it back and forth, pulling with all his
strength. Blood bubbled up as it came free
of the wound. "Mind out of the way," Cosmo
called, throwing the panel to the ground.

"The meglaphant's pulse is still weak,

Master Cosmo," Brain-E called up, its probe pushed against the beast's flank. "We must staunch the flow of blood from that wound."

"I'm on to it," Cosmo replied, unclipping a gun-like gadget from his utility belt and attaching it to his wrist. He switched it on, and it glowed with a purple light.

"Is that a UV welder?" Ranger Cron called up curiously. "Isn't that for welding burst pipes in spaceship engines?"

"I'm hoping its heat will make the leaking blood coagulate," Cosmo replied, kneeling beside the wound. He grabbed hold of the skin around the gash and pulled

it together, pointing the purple UV light at the wound. The blood started turning sticky like toffee, then hard, drying on the fur. "It's working!" he called down, seeing the gash crisping over like a scab.

"Vital signs stabilizing," Brain-E replied.

"No remaining blood loss," Cosmo confirmed. "That should do it."

Ranger Cron stroked the beast's cheek, smiling. "Thank you," he said.

Cosmo switched off the UV welder and climbed down. "She'll need plenty of rest but she's out of danger now." He felt anger welling up inside him as he realized how close Tanka had come to killing the meglaphant. He called to Nuri: "Any sign of the invader?"

Nuri was a short distance away, peering through her hawk-eye monocular at the huge stone pyramid portals at the edge of the landing area. "Not at the moment, but his attack seems to have continued over there," she replied, pointing towards them.

Brain-E bleeped nervously. "Those portals are the access routes into the other dimensions of the Life Sanctuary," it said.

Ranger Cron frowned. "The alien may have used one of the portals to enter another dimension. It could still be on the rampage in another part of the sanctuary."

"Nuri, Brain-E, let's go! We've an alien to stop," Cosmo said. "Goodbye, Ranger Cron."

Nuri latched Brain-E onto her wrist and they pushed their way through the fleeing beasts, past flattened jeeps, jetbikes and other ranger patrol vehicles.

Cosmo noticed ruts in the ground like those made by a tank's caterpillar tracks. "Brain-E, can you run a scan on these?"

The brainbot shone its laser scanner over the ground. "I'm picking up traces of metallicon sludge," it replied. "These were definitely made by the invader."

Cosmo followed Tanka's trail under an

archway, then between the huge pyramid portals. He glanced up in awe at the damage done: nearly all the pyramids' tops or sides had been blasted away, and Tanka's trail stopped at the entrance to the only portal that remained intact. As Cosmo approached, large stone doors slid open, revealing a glowing chamber inside. "Tanka must have entered this one and switched dimensions," he said.

"We should message all personnel in the Life Sanctuary to warn them," Nuri said, unclipping her communicator from her belt.

"Negative, Miss Nuri," Brain-E told her. "It's impossible to communicate between dimensions."

The G-Watch agents entered the portal, and Cosmo saw that the strange glow was coming from symbols engraved on the walls. "What are these, Brain-E?" he asked.

"Each symbol denotes a dimension of the sanctuary," Brain-E replied. The brainbot scuttled across the symbols, scanning them, and stopped on a symbol of a cloud. "I'm detecting traces of metallicon sludge on this one, as if Tanka has touched it."

"OK, hold tight," Nuri said, reaching out and touching it too. Suddenly the doors closed and a white light filled the portal.

Cosmo couldn't see a thing: no Nuri, no floor, no walls. He heard a low hum and the white light turned to darkness. "What's going on?"

"There's nothing to worry about, Master

Cosmo," Brain-E said from close by. "We're about to travel between dimensions."

Cosmo tried to reply, but he couldn't even hear his own voice. He felt dizzy, like he was spinning; it was as if he was fading in and out of consciousness. He felt a jolt, then steadied himself as the dark turned to light again, revealing the portal's stone exit wall sliding open.

"We've arrived," Brain-E said. "We've entered a new dimension of the sanctuary."

CHAPTER THREE

A NEW DIMENSION

Cosmo blinked in astonishment as he stepped from the portal onto a coral island floating in the sky. Clouds drifted past, and among them he could see hundreds more coral islands floating like multi-coloured balloons, with coral bridges spanning the gaps between them. It looked surreal! Cosmo stepped across the coral and felt himself bouncing as he walked in weak gravity. Holding onto the

trunk of a coral tree to steady himself, he
noticed brightly coloured coral flowers,
and fish darting between them. *Fish?* He
blinked again, not believing what his eyes
were telling him. But the flying creatures
were definitely fish, swimming in the air.
"Where exactly are we?" he exclaimed.

Brain-E bleeped by his feet. "Technically
we are still on Planet Kefu," the brainbot

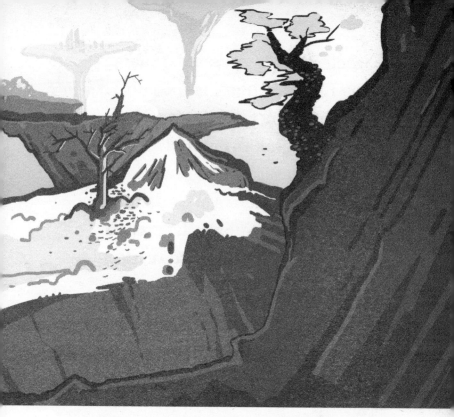

said. "But in a new dimension. According to my databank, this is dimension K17: rich in oxygenated vapour with near zero gravity. It's the Life Sanctuary's habitat for aero-aquatics."

"Aero-aquatics?"

"Cloud swimmers," Nuri explained, pointing to the fish in the sky. "Once native to the Dolie Vapour Worlds – before the whole place evaporated, that is."

"The Life Sanctuary is the only reason they're not extinct," Brain-E added.

"And now Tanka's entered their one surviving habitat," Cosmo said grimly. He noticed broken chunks of coral floating in the air, and cracks along the ground where the huge invader had trundled his way across. "We'd better hurry up and catch him!"

"Careful as you go," Nuri said. "One slip and it will be a slow, endless fall."

"I'll try my best," Cosmo gulped.

The three friends set off in pursuit of the invader, bouncing in K17's near-zero gravity. Cosmo pushed aside orange sunweed that was trailing from the branches of a coral tree, then ducked as a shoal of red-spotted fish burst from a cloud overhead. Where Tanka had smashed the corals, creatures had been disturbed: star urchins, anenomites, little micefish – these were attracting bigger fish hoping for an easy meal. Sky-eels snaked past Cosmo's legs, gobbling up tiny pink petal fish that swarmed together for protection, and a large black-winged ray glided low over the corals, sucking up hopping weedfrogs.

Nuri pulled Cosmo close, pointing up at large, fearsome creatures circling among the clouds overhead. "Stratosharx," she said. "We'd better stay alert. Tanka's destruction is upsetting the food chain."

Cosmo hurried onto the bridge that led to the next island. Between passing clouds he saw that parts of it were crumbling – it had clearly cracked under Tanka's weight.

"Don't look down," Brain-E advised from behind him.

Cosmo peeked over the bridge's side – but soon wished he hadn't. It was mind-blowing realizing how high he was; the cloudy sky seemed to extend into infinity in all directions – up, down and around.

Cosmo fixed his gaze on the bridge and, as another cloud engulfed him, he stepped blindly across it. He breathed a sigh of relief as he reached the next island. But as the cloud cleared, a distant *BOOM!* sounded, causing the fish to scatter.

"What was that?" Nuri asked, peering into the distance. There came three more explosions, one after the other: *BOOM! . . . BOOM! . . . BOOM! . . .*

"It has to be Tanka!" Cosmo said. "Hurry!"

Cosmo, Nuri and Brain-E picked up the pace, crossing the island and the next bridge in long bouncing strides. Soon the air was thick with floating coral debris, and the bellows of a creature in distress echoed through the sky. Cosmo saw writhing tentacles amongst the wreckage of a smashed coral reef.

"Oh my, it's a decapus!" Nuri said worriedly. "Tanka's destroyed its home."

"Please be careful. Decapi are extremely dangerous when angry," Brain-E warned.

But there was no way around the creature, so they had to continue warily past it. They ducked as a thick suckered tentacle whipped towards them, then scrambled between two more that were thrashing in the air. Through the debris, Cosmo glimpsed two bulbous yellow eyes and a mouth full of teeth. Tentacles lashed

around them, coiling into the sky and swinging overhead, sending broken coral clattering against their visors. A tentacle coiled around Cosmo's helmet, its thick suckers throbbing against his visor.

Nuri dragged him away. "Keep moving!" she called above the beast's angry bellows.

Dodging more tentacles, they reached the far side of the island. But where the bridge should have been they saw only floating chunks of coral among the clouds.

"Tanka's blown the bridge!" Cosmo said, holding weed growing from a coral tree to steady himself.

"We have to find a way to follow him," Nuri said in alarm.

Cosmo glanced up at a large black-winged ray swimming overhead. "Ready to hitch a ride?" he asked Nuri.

"Oh, surely not!" Brain-E said, gripping Nuri's arm tightly.

Nuri smiled. "One . . . two . . . three!"

Cosmo and Nuri leaped up into the sky. They rose in the weak gravity and grabbed hold of the ray's fins, pulling themselves onto its back.

Cosmo knelt upright, stroking the ray's smooth skin reassuringly. It was like being on a flying carpet – the huge fish had enormous wing-like fins and a tail like a rudder. It flew gracefully through the cloudy sky, away from the angry decapus,

weaving between the debris of the destroyed coral islands and bridges.

"Tanka, we're coming to get you!" Nuri called, clinging on tightly.

As the ray flew through the thick cloud, its gills opened and closed, breathing the cloud's water vapour. Cosmo and Nuri held on tightly, flying blind until they emerged into a patch of open sky where they saw more floating islands that were still intact. On one of them stood another pyramid portal. "My guess is that Tanka has used that portal and switched dimensions again," Cosmo said.

As they flew above the pyramid, Cosmo, Nuri and Brain-E jumped off, falling slowly in the weak gravity and landing on the island with a soft bump. Sure enough, the ground was cracked, as if something huge had trundled across it. As Cosmo approached, the portal doors slid open and he stepped inside the pyramid and looked around at the glowing symbols. "Brain-E, can you tell which dimension Tanka chose?"

Brain-E scurried up onto the wall, scanning the symbols for traces of Tanka's metallicon sludge. "This one," it said, scuttling over to a symbol that looked like jagged teeth. "The prehistoric dimension."

"Prehistoric?"

"A land of monsters," Brain-E explained.

"Monsters! That's all we need!" Cosmo took a deep breath, then pressed the symbol. Bright light filled the portal, then a hum sounded and darkness descended as they began travelling between dimensions.

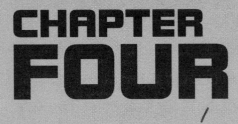

CHAPTER
FOUR

MONSTERS

The portal doors slid open and Cosmo stepped cautiously into a new dimension: a rocky plateau where a sulphurous stench filled his nostrils. He quickly closed his visor to keep out the acrid gas, and looked out over a fiery landscape of bubbling lava lakes, smoking sulphur marshes and craggy mountains. Roaming the land were giant reptilian monsters.

Brain-E bleeped from the ground. "This

is dimension K19: a prehistoric dimension,
home to some of the first galactic species,
now extinct in all other realms."

Cosmo noticed Tanka's tracks on the
dry cracked ground, leading away from
the plateau towards the hotter lowlands.

"Tanka's here for sure," he said, heading off in pursuit.

"Hey, Cosmo, these might help," Nuri called. She'd spotted two sanctuary trailerbikes abandoned beside the pyramid. Each had a rear trailer with a crate on it.

Cosmo dashed back and opened one of the crates to see what was inside. "They're full of raw meat," he said, prodding the pile of juicy steaks inside.

"The rangers must have been about to feed the beasts when Tanka turned up," Nuri commented.

"I hope they made it out safely," Cosmo said. He climbed onto a bike and kick-started its engine. "Come on, let's get after this alien."

Nuri climbed onto the other bike and Brain-E scuttled onto its handlebars, clinging on tightly. They sped away down the slope onto the lowlands and rode

along the dry shore of a vast, red-hot lava
lake, following Tanka's caterpillar tracks
in the steaming cracked ground.

A giant prehistoric turtle was pulling
itself out of the lava onto the shore as
they approached. Its smooth shell glowed
red from the heat and its skin dripped
with lava as it opened its mouth,
lumbering slowly towards them.

"It's a lavatugo," Brain-E said. "And it
looks like it's come to be fed."

Cosmo reached round and flipped the lid off his crate. He grabbed a steak and hurled it towards the creature. The lavatugo lunged for the meat, snapping its jaws, and gobbled the steak down whole.

"Hungry thing," Cosmo said, speeding away.

"There are creatures here with much larger appetites than that," Brain-E replied ominously.

Cosmo followed Tanka's trail into a yellow mist and felt his trailerbike skidding, its wheels sliding on the wet ground of a sulphur marsh. Suddenly a vast eight-legged beast appeared, its head and upper body lost high in the mist.

"A bull-megakron!" Brain-E cried.

Cosmo swerved to avoid the beast's huge foot as it came thumping down in the sulphur marsh, splashing yellow acidic water. He twisted the trailerbike's throttle, accelerating alongside Nuri beneath the prehistoric monster's fat belly, then veered sharply aside, just avoiding another huge foot as they sped out the other side.

"That was close," Nuri said.

Just then Cosmo heard a boom from up ahead and felt the ground shake beneath the wheels of his bike.

"Sounds like something being blasted!" Nuri called to him, her sensitive Etrusian hearing identifying the sound as cannon fire. "Tanka must be near."

Cosmo opened his bike's throttle and sped out of the sulphur mist. He saw a range of craggy mountains, and a flock of sulphurdactyls flying overhead, squawking in panic as they escaped from the blast. He hurried along Tanka's trail, bumping over the churned ground towards a dry ravine in the mountains. It had sheer slopes on either side and was blocked by a huge rockfall, dust still swirling in the air.

Cosmo and Nuri skidded to a stop.

"Tanka's brought down the mountainside!" Nuri said in shock.

"That's not all he's destroyed. Look," Cosmo said, pointing up to eggs the size of barrels lying smashed amongst the rubble, their orange yolks oozing down. Near the top of the rockfall, he noticed the twisted branches of a huge nest from where the eggs must have fallen.

Brain-E bleeped nervously. "Oh goodness, it's a rocmadox nest. We mustn't linger here any longer. Rocmadox are fearsome, territorial creatures. If there's one nearby we could be in danger."

"Follow me," Nuri announced. She twisted her bike's accelerator and sped straight up the jagged rockfall, steering skillfully, her rear wheel spraying dust and stones as she went.

Cosmo watched, impressed, as she rode over the peak. Not wanting to be outdone, he sped after her, standing up on his footgrips as his bike climbed. As he reached the top of the rockfall, he spotted one rocmadox egg that was still intact, half buried in the rubble, and got off his bike to dig it out. "Hold on, I think I can rescue one of these eggs before the rocks slide again."

Nuri was waiting for Cosmo beyond the rockfall, down in the ravine. Brain-E's lights flashed nervously from her handlebars. "That may not be a good idea, Master Cosmo," it said. "If a mother rocmadox is nearby and sees you with her egg, she may not take kindly towards you."

"I'll just move it to safety," Cosmo replied, heaving rocks away from the egg and lifting it up in his arms. The egg felt warm, and he carried it across the rockfall to a ledge in the wall of the ravine where its mother could find it easily. But just as he put the egg down, he heard an angry hissing sound from above. He looked up and saw a huge horn-headed lizard climbing down the side of the mountain towards him.

"I was just rescuing your egg," Cosmo called to it, edging gradually away. But the rocmadox snarled, revealing dozens of sharp teeth. A whip-like tongue flicked out of its mouth, lashing Cosmo and

sending him staggering backwards onto the rocks.

"Cosmo, time to move!" Nuri cried from below. She threw a meaty steak to distract the rocmadox. As the beast snatched it up, Cosmo scrambled onto his bike and sped down the rockfall, racing away with Nuri along the ravine. The huge lizard gave chase.

"So you like meat, do you?" Cosmo called back to it. He flipped open the crate on the trailer of his bike, then called to Nuri: "Hold steady – I'm going to hitch a ride with you!" Cosmo stood up on the seat of his bike and let go of the handlebars.

"Cosmo, are you crazy?" Nuri called.

He leaped from his bike to Nuri's, landing behind her on her seat, leaving his bike to swerve away riderless and crash into the side of the ravine.

Raw meat spilled out of its crate and

the rocmadox set upon it hungrily,
abandoning the chase to eat its fill.

"Nice move, Master Cosmo," Brain-E
said.

Nuri smiled. "You *are* crazy."

Having escaped the rocmadox, Cosmo

and Nuri continued on Tanka's trail, following the invader's tracks to the end of the ravine, where another huge pyramid portal stood.

Cosmo jumped off the trailerbike and hurried into the portal. "Where's Tanka headed now, Brain-E?" he asked, looking at the glowing symbols carved into the stone.

Brain-E scuttled up the wall and scanned the symbols for metallicon slime. He stopped on a symbol of a ghoulish face, its mouth open wide in a scream. "Oh dear, I don't like the look of this," the brainbot said. "It's the nether dimension."

"The nether dimension? What's that?" Cosmo asked.

Brain-E didn't reply but tapped the symbol. A white light engulfed them, then came a hum, then darkness and silence.

Cosmo felt his head spin, and he drifted in and out of consciousness as they travelled between dimensions. With a sudden jolt, they arrived at their destination. But the light didn't return this time; as the portal's exit slid open, an inky black darkness remained. Cosmo felt chills running up and down his spine.

Brain-E bleeped and its voice quivered: "M-Master Cosmo, do be careful here. The nether dimension is home to the paranormals."

CHAPTER FIVE

INTO THE NIGHT

The nether dimension was a dark place,
darker than the blackest night, and
ghostly groans came from all around.
Cosmo fumbled for the plasma torch on
his utility belt, and switched it on as he
stepped from the portal, its beam
illuminating the trees of a forest. He
heard the sounds of creatures swinging
and scurrying away through the
branches.

"Switch it off!" Brain-E said urgently. "Many of the paranormals that live in this dimension are sensitive to light."

Cosmo quickly switched off his torch and instead spoke a command into the voice sensor of his helmet: "Night vision." His visor adjusted, revealing the forest to him in a grainy infra-red image.

Nuri switched her goggles to night-vision too, then clambered over a fallen tree to inspect the ground beyond it. It was churned up by caterpillar tracks. "Tanka's definitely been this way," she said.

Cosmo scrambled after her. "What *are* paranormals, Brain-E?" he asked nervously.

"Life forms such as ghost variants, ether creatures, skeletoids and zombie trees."

"Sounds like a Halloween nightmare!" Cosmo said. "I'm guessing it's dangerous here too, right?"

"Yes, Master Cosmo. I would advise extreme caution."

Cosmo frowned as a thought occurred to him. "Brain-E, are all the Life Sanctuary's dimensions dangerous?" he asked.

Brain-E's lights flashed. "Not all, Master Cosmo. Most are quite safe."

"It's like Tanka's deliberately targeting the deadliest parts of the sanctuary," Cosmo replied.

"He must know we're after him," Nuri said. "He's trying to scare us off."

"Well, it won't work." Cosmo tried to sound braver than he felt.

But as they tracked the invader through the forest, an icy wind whistled past them, and ghostly groans mingled with the creaking and scraping of the trees' leafless branches, setting Cosmo's nerves on edge. Spots of red flickered among the dark trees, and out of the corner of his visor Cosmo glimpsed dozens of red eyes watching them. When he turned to get a closer look, they seemed to blink and were gone. "We're being watched," he whispered nervously.

"They're phantomangi," Brain-E explained. "Shadow creatures that prey on the life-force of others."

There came a piercing shriek overhead and Cosmo heard the phantomangi scattering through the trees.

"Don't look up, Cosmo!" Nuri warned. "That shriek was from a nightwarbler. It's bad luck to see a nightwarbler."

"Bad luck?" Cosmo asked, glimpsing the luminous shape of a phantom bird hovering above the treetops. Suddenly he felt dread in the pit of his stomach, as if bad luck was seeping into him. *That's all I need!* he thought. "Come on, let's get out of here!"

The G-Watch agents pressed onwards after Tanka. Cosmo felt goosebumps prickling his skin, and chills running up and down his spine. A green mist was gathering. He heard Nuri's teeth chattering. "Are you OK, Nuri?" he asked.

"I th-th-think so," she replied. But as the green mist enveloped them, he could see her blue skin turning frosty pale.

"It's an ether creature surrounding us," Brain-E said from the forest floor, scanning the mist with a probe arm. "It's a mist beast that feeds on its prey by paralysing it with fright then digesting it over a period of weeks. Don't worry, Miss Nuri. You are too big for it to take hold."

"That's g-good to know," Nuri replied, shaking herself to get rid of the goosebumps and pushing on.

"This place is *way* creepy," Cosmo said. The mist drifted away, and the ether creature moved off in search of a more manageable snack. They hurried onwards to a group of larger fallen trees where Tanka had crashed through. Cosmo, Nuri and Brain-E had to clamber over them, scrambling between broken branches that were oozing sticky sap. The trees seemed more gnarled than the others in the forest. Cosmo's Quantum Mutation Suit snagged on a branch, then his boot went right through a rotten trunk. As Nuri reached back to help him free himself, the tree shuddered and groaned.

Cosmo leaped aside, horrified, and the tree rose from the ground, pushing itself up on its twisted branches. Along its rough trunk, green eyes blinked open and it pulled its roots out of the soil like legs. The tree towered over Cosmo, groaning and moaning, its branches outstretched like horrifying arms. More trees, each just as rotten and deformed, began pulling up their roots and gathering around the G-Watch team.

"These are zombie trees from the galaxy's lost worlds!" Brain-E said. "According to my databank, a once-extinct

species re-grown in the sanctuary from fossilized DNA."

"Why would anyone want to grow these scary things?" Cosmo asked, stepping back fearfully as the trees encircled them.

"Its the sanctuary's aim to maintain a living example of *all* galactic life forms," Brain-E added. "DNA from each and every one is stored in the sanctuary's scientific Hub."

"DNA from every living thing in the

galaxy?" Cosmo asked, a worrying thought occurring to him. "And what if the Hub were to be destroyed?"

"It would be a catastrophe," Brain-E replied. "The backup for all galactic life would be lost."

"I hate to interrupt, but we're being surrounded," Nuri said, pulling her phaser gun from her utility belt and setting it to stun mode. But one of the

zombie trees whipped out a branch and knocked the gun from her hand.

The strange creatures were closing in on all sides, trying to block their escape. "Run for it!" Cosmo cried.

Cosmo, Nuri and Brain-E darted for gaps between the creatures, but a root shot out, clutching hold of Cosmo's right ankle, and he stumbled and fell on his face. "Aargh!"

Nuri was grabbed too, roots writhing around her, binding her tightly.

"Miss Nuri, Master Cosmo, are you OK?!" Brain-E called, scuttling to their aid. But a branch reached down and snatched the brainbot, lifting it up high.

"Brain-E, where did you go?" Cosmo said, panicking. He struggled as another root grabbed his left ankle. He could feel his legs being pulled from beneath him. "Heeelp!"

CHAPTER SIX

KAOS

Beyond the galaxy, on the battleship
Oblivion, the five-headed outlaw Kaos
faced a bank of monitors, checking
images, graphs and charts displaying the
vital functions of the metallicon Tanka.
His five heads leaned in.

"Pulse regular," the first head said.

"Engine revs high," the second added.

"Brain waves strong," said the third.

"Ammunition plentiful," said the fourth.

"Excellent!" exclaimed his fifth head.
It turned to look at a purple rat that was
cleaning its whiskers by the monitors.
"Wugrat, tune in to Tanka's ocular
camera. Let's see what he's looking at!"

Wugrat scraped a switch with its
claws, and on one of the monitors an
image of a pulsing white light appeared.

"Splendid." The fifth head grinned.
"Tanka is travelling between dimensions

on his way to the Life Sanctuary's Hub."

"He'll blow the Hub to smithereens," Kaos's first head said excitedly.

"And thousands of species in the galaxy will become vulnerable to extinction," the second head added.

"Fear and panic will spread and G-Watch will be forced to surrender to our demands."

"Eeek, eek, eeeeek," Wugrat interrupted, whiskers twitching anxiously.

"Oh, Wugrat, will you stop worrying about G-Watch's meddling Agent Supreme," the fifth head said. "This time we'll not fail because *I* have thought of the perfect plan: I have programmed that metal-head Tanka to lead those G-Watch agents into deadly peril, so the Earthling boy won't make it as far as the Hub – he'll be dead before he even has the chance to fight Tanka!"

All five heads grinned at once. "Victory will be ours!"

Back in the Life Sanctuary's nether dimension, one of the zombie trees' branches grabbed hold of Cosmo, lifting him off the ground.

"Whoooaaaaaaaa!" he cried, trying not to panic as he felt himself being passed upwards from branch to branch, dozens of green eyes staring at him.

The zombie tree's rotting trunk split open like a huge mouth, and Cosmo saw bugs, maggots and spiders inside among the decomposing compost of the tree's past prey. *It's the creature's feeding hole*, he realized. And he was being bundled towards it! Cosmo kicked and struggled, but the branches held him firmly.

"Master Cosmo, help!" he heard a voice call over his helmet's earpiece. It was Brain-E!

"Where are you, Brain-E?" Cosmo replied urgently into his mic.

"I'm inside the trunk!" came the reply.

Oh no, Cosmo thought, *Brain-E's in that lot somewhere.* Trying to avoid being pushed inside too, he reached his arm into the tree's rotting mouth. "I'll get you out, Brain-E!" he called, searching desperately for the brainbot.

"Shine your torch, Master Cosmo!" Brain-E said.

"It's OK, I can see with my visor's night vision."

"Master Cosmo, shine your torch!"

"Don't worry, Brain-E—"

"Cosmo, listen," Nuri's voice interrupted over his earpiece. "Brain-E's trying to help!"

Cosmo glanced down and spotted Nuri pinned to the forest floor, roots wound around her. She was trying to reach for her plasma torch but her arms were bound too tightly.

"Cosmo, zombie trees don't like the light!" she called. "Shine your torch!"

Realizing what Nuri and Brain-E were trying to tell him, Cosmo quickly switched on his plasma torch. Just as he was being pushed inside the mouth, he shone the beam at the tree's trunk. Dozens of green eyes blinked and the tree roared in shock, its mouth stretching wide.

Cosmo felt himself tumbling out again, along with thousands of bugs, maggots, spiders – and Brain-E! He bumped and crashed down through the branches. "Whoaah . . . ouch . . . eeaaay . . . Oooof!" He landed in a heap in the mud beside Nuri, then came Brain-E, then a hail of insects pouring down on their heads.

Other trees reached down, trying to snatch them again, but Cosmo shone his plasma torch into their eyes, causing them to recoil and release Nuri too. "Now, let's get out of here!" he said, scooping up Brain-E so the brainbot could wrap itself around his wrist, then shining his torch to open a gap in the circle of trees.

Cosmo and Nuri sprinted away, racing between the retreating trees, Cosmo's torch beam clearing the way.

"We must try to find Tanka's trail," Nuri called.

"But I can't tell which way he went," Cosmo said: the trampled zombie trees had moved since the invader passed by.

"To your right!" Nuri yelled, and Cosmo's torch beam shone on a sloping stone wall beyond the branches. It was a pyramid portal! They ran over and hurried inside to safety.

"That was *not* fun!" Cosmo said, flicking maggots off his spacesuit.

Brain-E quickly detached itself from his wrist and scurried up the stone wall, scanning the glowing symbols. "I'm detecting metallicon slime here," the brainbot said, pointing to an engraved X.

"And what dimension is that?"

"X marks the centre of the Life Sanctuary, the site of the Hub."

"Where the galaxy's DNA is stored?" Cosmo asked, concerned.

"Affirmative. Tanka has entered the most vital part of the Life Sanctuary."

Cosmo slammed his hand on the symbol, and white light surrounded them, along with a low hum. Then silence descended and the light turned to darkness. Dizziness came next as they pulsed in and out of consciousness, journeying to the dimension marked X. With a sudden jolt they arrived and the exit opened. Cosmo stepped out into golden daylight, high up among mountains. Ahead, a track wound down towards a vast scientific facility, its buildings gleaming in the light from three golden suns. "The Hub!" Cosmo said.

Around the pyramid portal, rangers' buggies and jetbikes lay abandoned, some squashed flat; caterpillar tracks marked the ground. Cosmo heard an engine roar and looked to his left. On the mountain ridge along from the pyramid stood a terrifying alien: a living war machine at least ten metres tall. The invader was positioned like a sniper, its

mighty cannon arm pointing down into
the valley.

"It's Tanka!"

"And he's going to blast the Hub!" Nuri
exclaimed.

As she spoke there came a *BOOM!* –
Tanka's cannon arm let loose a mighty

neutron blast, and one of the Hub's surveillance towers exploded, toppling over as the blast hit. *BOOM!* The invader let loose another, taking out a domed building inside the Hub.

Cosmo gasped, seeing lab personnel running for cover. "Nuri, get down there and evacuate everyone," he instructed. "I'll deal with Tanka!"

"Are you sure you're ready for this, Cosmo?" Nuri asked anxiously.

Cosmo summoned his courage and felt his power surge through his tired limbs, activating his Quantum Mutation Suit, causing it to ripple with blue light. "You bet, Nuri! It's mutation time!"

As Nuri leaped onto a jetbike and sped off with Brain-E down the mountain, Cosmo climbed up onto an upturned buggy where he could be seen. "Hey, tin machine! Over here!" he shouted to Tanka.

The alien swung his cannon arm

round, pointing it towards Cosmo. "You're meant to be DEAD, Earth boy!" he bellowed. *BOOM!*

Tanka fired a neutron blast and Cosmo dived for cover as the buggy exploded. "SCAN!" he said into his helmet's voice sensor. Images of aliens appeared on the visor's digital display: a diamond-eyed shrill . . . a mountain grunx . . . a noxious tentacula . . . Cosmo scrolled through them, comparing their features. *What alien can take on a living tank?* he wondered. He stopped on an image of a purple winged creature. It looked muscular, like a cross between a gargoyle and an ogre.

NAME: DARE-X
SPECIES: POWERGOYLE
ORIGIN: RAVINES OF GROL
HEIGHT: 8 METRES
WEIGHT: 5.3 TONNES
FEATURE: POWER OF A FLYING CANNONBALL

Dare-X will be too powerful for Tanka, Cosmo thought. *That junk heap won't know what hit him!* "MUTATE!"

CHAPTER SEVEN

DARE-X

Cosmo's body tingled as his spacesuit
fused with his flesh. His molecular
pattern began to reconfigure: his skin
turned leathery and stretched as his
muscles expanded; his shoulder blades
split through his back, growing into
powergoyle wings. Soon he was over
six times his normal size and bursting
with the explosive power of a flying
cannonball.

"An Earthling can't beat me!" he heard Tanka roar.

Cosmo beat his powergoyle wings, breaking cover. "But a powergoyle might!" he yelled confidently.

As Tanka launched a volley of neutron blasts – *BOOM! BOOM! BOOM!* – Cosmo began his attack too, and in a blur of beating wings he unleashed himself along the mountain ridge towards the mighty invader, half flying and half bounding. His muscular powergoyle legs leaped from rock to rock as he weaved and dodged to avoid the cannon fire.

"I'll blow you to pieces!" Tanka bellowed, swivelling his gun this way

then that, trying to keep Dare-X in his sights. The invader revved his engines, increasing the pressure in his neutron gun chamber. *BOOM! BOOM! BOOM!*

With a swift beat of his wings, Cosmo zipped to his right, then his left to avoid the blasts once again. "Too slow," he jeered as the ground exploded behind him.

Smoke and dust swirled on the ridge, cloaking the golden sunlight. Tanka fired again and again, but Cosmo zigzagged, agile and strong, more than a match for the lumbering metallicon. With a somersault, Cosmo leaped over Tanka's cannon arm and onto his back. "Gotcha!" he cried, reaching round and covering Tanka's eyes.

Tanka shook his head angrily. "What the—" *BOOM! BOOM!* The alien's gun swivelled wildly, shooting blindly along the smoky ridge.

As Dare-X, Cosmo was less than half

the size of Tanka, but he was still strong.
He punched dents in Tanka's armour,
then zipped round and grabbed hold of
the alien's cannon arm. He swung it to the
side, pointing it well away from the Hub.

But Tanka still had his right arm free,
complete with its hydraulic gripping claw.
He got hold of Cosmo, pulling him off his
cannon and hurling him to the ground.

Cosmo shuddered as his head hit a
rock and a wave of dizziness washed
over him. He tried to get to his feet, but
felt his powergoyle strength waning. He
looked up fearfully and saw the mighty
silhouette of Tanka bearing down on him.
Cosmo just managed to roll himself into
a protective ball and tense his muscles as
Tanka's caterpillar tracks rolled straight
over him.

"Ha! Looks like you're flat out there!"
Tanka said, leaving Cosmo for dead as he
drove on down the mountainside.

Cosmo's powergoyle body was
crumpled and aching, his wings broken
and his bones shattered. He was no

match for Tanka's size and brute strength. "RESET," he said, feeling his flesh tingle and his wounds heal as he shrank back into an Earthling boy.

He glanced down the mountainside and saw Tanka crashing through the Hub's perimeter gates, and Kefuan rangers fleeing on buggies. Only one person seemed prepared to face the invader: Nuri, riding out on the jetbike firing her phaser gun at Tanka.

The invader unleashed a neutron blast back at her. *BOOM!* It slammed into her path and her bike skidded, sending her tumbling to the ground.

Cosmo leaped to his feet and raced down the mountain towards her. "SCAN!" he said into his helmet's sensor. As he ran, digital images of aliens scrolled across the visor of his Quantum Mutation Suit . . . a shrieking dilkon . . . a radioactive snart . . . an eight-horned guka.

I need something that can take on that metallicon at close range, he thought, bounding over the debris of the perimeter gates. He searched for the strongest, largest alien he could find . . .

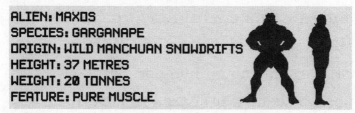

ALIEN: MAXOS
SPECIES: GARGANAPE
ORIGIN: WILD MANCHUAN SNOWDRIFTS
HEIGHT: 37 METRES
WEIGHT: 20 TONNES
FEATURE: PURE MUSCLE

Maxos will make tinfoil out of Tanka, Cosmo thought. He spoke into the helmet's voice sensor: "MUTATE!"

CHAPTER
EIGHT

MAXOS

Cosmo's power surged and he felt his whole body tingle as he began to mutate. Coarse black hair sprouted from his skin, and his face and body twisted into that of a garganape. His muscles bulged as he grew outwards and upwards, getting bigger . . . and bigger . . . and bigger. He was Maxos!

Tall and mighty, Cosmo strode through the Hub's compound, towering over the smashed Kefuan vehicles that littered the way. "Stop right there, Tanka!" he bellowed.

Tanka turned towards Cosmo and looked up at him in surprise, but before the invader had time to fire, Cosmo bore down on him in a single huge stride. Maxos had long arms and massive hands; he reached down and grasped Tanka's cannon arm, pushing it aside.

BOOM! The neutron blast fired harmlessly into the side of the valley.

Tanka bunched his hydraulic claw into a fist and tried to swing it at Cosmo, but Cosmo just grabbed it and squeezed, hearing a crunch as the metallicon's claw was crushed.

"It's time to finish this," Cosmo boomed. Holding Tanka with both hands, he lifted him off the ground.

"Let go of me!" Tanka roared.

Cosmo's garganape muscles bulged as he raised the invader above his head. "And

don't come back," he said, hurling Tanka
high over the Hub's perimeter fence.

The invader smashed down onto the

ground, his armoured plating crumpled, his cannon arm bent. His eye-lights flickered, then went dark.

Cosmo glanced around, looking for Nuri and Brain-E. He saw Nuri back on her jetbike, riding out from behind a wrecked truck with Brain-E on the bike's handlebars.

"Nice one, Cosmo!" she called.

He was just about to give her a thumbs-up when he heard the sound of grinding metal and the roar of an engine starting up.

"Uh-oh, I spoke too soon!" Nuri called again.

Cosmo turned back and saw the invader stirring, his eye-lights flickering back on, silver metallic slime bubbling around his broken casing and soldering the cracks in his bodywork. His claw-hand reached round and untwisted his bent cannon arm, pointing it straight at Cosmo. "That makes me mad!" Tanka hollered.

BOOM! A blast of neutron energy burst from the invader's cannon, slamming into Cosmo's chest, knocking him off his feet. As Maxos, Cosmo toppled with the force of a huge tree and went crashing backwards onto a laboratory building, the impact smashing through the roof and shattering the windows.

Cosmo lay amongst the rubble, hardly able to breathe, feeling a pain in his chest where the neutron blast had hit him. "RESET," he gasped. His garganape body tingled as his wounds healed and he turned back into his boy self once again. He looked up wearily, only to see Tanka smashing through the perimeter fence back into the Hub compound, his cannon arm pointing straight at Cosmo once more.

"I've had enough of your meddling, Freak Boy!" Tanka roared.

Cosmo braced himself for the blast, but instead heard the hum of a jetbike as

Nuri rode across the compound at top speed and steered between him and Tanka, heading straight for the invader. "Nobody hurts my friend and gets away with it!" she yelled.

"Nuri, stop!" Cosmo called, but she was on a collision course with the alien.

Tanka laughed. "Ha! You're not even worth a blast of my gun. I'll just roll straight over you instead!" His engines roared and he powered towards her, his caterpillar tracks spinning.

But with Tanka about to run her over, Nuri flicked the jetbike's handlebars, causing it to lean to one side and skid along the ground, sliding into the gap between the alien's two caterpillar treads. Nuri unclipped two gravity grenades from her utility belt and reached up, fixing them to Tanka's undercarriage, then slid out at the alien's rear. Tanka reached round, trying to grab her with his hydraulic claw, but Nuri was too fast and sped away to the shelter of a laboratory building where Brain-E was waiting for her.

Brilliant! Cosmo thought, rushing to grab hold of the building too, aware of what the gravity grenades would do to anything that wasn't fastened down.

With a muffled *THWUMP!* the gravity grenades exploded beneath the invader,

sending Tanka upwards, spinning over and over, floating weightlessly, high in the air. Throughout the valley, gravity weakened, and huge rocks, vehicles and debris rose off the ground. Suddenly the sky was full of objects slowly spinning in the low gravity. Then, once the effect of the blast had worn off, they came crashing back to the ground. Tanka thudded down heavily, nuts and bolts bursting from him, his caterpillar tracks buckling as he landed.

For a moment there was silence.

Cosmo waited anxiously, watching the invader. Tanka didn't move. Cosmo took a step towards him.

"Stay back, Master Cosmo," Brain-E called, scuttling out from the laboratory building with Nuri following. "I'll dismantle his circuits so he can't use his neutron blaster again!" The brave little robot scuttled up onto Tanka's gun nozzle and disappeared inside. But as it did so, the alien's engines roared back to life once more with a sickening splutter.

BOOM! Tanka blasted Brain-E out of his cannon arm, shooting the brainbot at one of the Hub's solar towers. The tower exploded, toppling in a cloud of dust, but to Cosmo's relief the brainbot's lights flashed among the rubble, signalling that it was still OK.

"Enough of these games!" Tanka bellowed, and with a roar of his engines the alien was on the move again, his buckled caterpillar tracks carrying him awkwardly over the rubble, advancing towards the huge industrial-size storage hangars in the centre of the Hub.

Nuri rushed to Cosmo's side. "He's heading towards the Hub's main buildings!" she cried. "Cosmo, you have to do something!"

BOOM! A neutron blast slammed into the side of the Hub's seed store, where a collection of seeds from all around the galaxy was housed. Cosmo ducked as millions of them, large and small, rattled down throughout the valley like hail.

BOOM! Tanka blasted a store of precious pollen, and fine powders billowed into the air like dazzling multicoloured fog.

BOOM! Tanka fired on a huge store of eggs from across the galaxy, and sticky yolk and chunks of shell rained down.

"Nothing can stop me!" the invader roared, powering towards a vast tower in the centre of the Hub.

"Quickly, Master Cosmo – that's the DNA store," Brain-E cried, scuttling back over to Cosmo and Nuri. "Inside is DNA belonging to every known species in the galaxy."

It's now or never, Cosmo thought. "SCAN!" he said into the sensor of his Quantum Mutation Suit.

CHAPTER
NINE

TERMAX FIGHTS BACK

Images of aliens scrolled across Cosmo's visor once again. He searched for an alien to beat Tanka once and for all. He noticed one that was altogether different: a tiny little alien creature with six legs and oversized jaws:

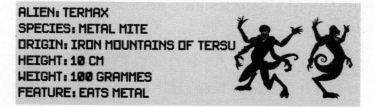

ALIEN: TERMAX
SPECIES: METAL MITE
ORIGIN: IRON MOUNTAINS OF TERSU
HEIGHT: 10 CM
WEIGHT: 100 GRAMMES
FEATURE: EATS METAL

Eats metal! Termax could gnaw his way inside Tanka, Cosmo thought. "MUTATE!"

Power surged through Cosmo's body once more, activating the Quantum Mutation Suit, and his every molecule began to vibrate. His head twisted and his jaws mutated into two rows of jagged, diamond-like teeth. He gnashed them together – they felt sharp. His arms and legs were now jointed like an insect's, two extra limbs sprouting from his sides. Then he began to shrink, getting smaller and smaller until he was the size of a large bug.

Cosmo scuttled after Tanka, running along the ground like a beetle. He leaped onto the back of the invader's caterpillar tracks and used their forward motion to carry him upwards. He jumped from one track onto Tanka's side and began gnawing his way through the invader's armour plating. As Termax, Cosmo was small but had a bite that could slice

through metal like butter. Cosmo
gnawed, nibbled and gnashed.

"Hey, stop that!" Tanka roared, trying
to see what was nibbling him. He reached
out with his hydraulic claw, but Cosmo
was too small for him to grab hold of.

With his metal mite jaws, Cosmo made
light work of Tanka's thick armour
plating and burrowed his way through to
the invader's insides.

"Hey, where did you go?" he heard
Tanka roar, as the invader prodded with

his hydraulic claw. But Cosmo was in amongst his inner workings, too deep for the alien to reach. It was almost dark inside the invader, and there was a strong smell of engine oil. Tanka's machinery was greased and hot from cannon fire.

Trying not to vomit, Cosmo munched his way through silver metallicon flesh, circuitry and wires, spitting out debris as he went. He gnawed through brake cables and engine pistons to reach Tanka's neutron reactor – the fuel chamber that powered the invader's cannon. Cosmo ate his way into the neutron reactor, causing its fuel to leak out and trickle through the machinery – fuel that would normally create the cannon's neutron blast. Cosmo nibbled and gnawed until the neutron chamber was riddled with holes. *If I'm right, when Tanka tries to ignite this fuel to fire his gun, it won't be his cannon that blasts*, Cosmo thought.

"I will destroy this place!" Tanka roared, his insides rumbling.

Cosmo quickly nibbled his way back out, exiting through the alien's undercarriage and dropping to the ground. He scuttled ahead of Tanka, positioning himself between the invader and the DNA store.

"RESET," Cosmo said, and his metal mite insect body mutated back into his regular humanoid form. His diamond-like teeth receded, and he stood before Tanka, a boy once more. The alien had a pained expression on his face. "What's wrong, Tanka? Got a tummy ache?" Cosmo asked.

Tanka was straining, clawing at his armour plating, trying to work out what had happened to his insides. "I'll blow you to pieces!" he bellowed at Cosmo.

"Give it your best shot then," Cosmo said. He stood firm, hands on hips, goading the alien to blast him. He crossed his fingers, hoping he'd done enough to disable the alien's weapon.

Nuri came running. "What are you doing, Cosmo? He'll destroy you *and* the Hub!"

Tanka's engines revved as he ignited his neutron chamber. "I WILL END YOU, EARTHLING!" he roared. But instead of a *BOOM!* of cannon fire, there came an almighty *WHUMPH!* from inside the invader. The leaking neutron fuel ignited and Tanka's metal body shuddered, his armour plating flying off in chunks and his caterpillar tracks shredding.

"NOOOO!" the invader roared, crumpling to the ground, smoke pouring

out of him. He tried in vain to trundle along on his broken tracks. One eye-light was hanging from its socket on a coiled wire. It flashed, then went out. Cosmo had done it! The alien had backfired!

"It's over, Tanka," Cosmo said, his brave power surging through him, causing his Quantum Mutation Suit to glow once more. From Cosmo's hand a beam of bright light extended – the power sword – the power inside him taking the form of a weapon.

Cosmo stepped towards the invader, climbing onto Tanka's broken chassis. Tanka tried to lift his hydraulic claw to swing at him, but it creaked and toppled as Cosmo struck the alien with the sword, sending his power into him. "The power of the universe will defeat you!" he cried.

Cosmo could feel his brave power battling the metallicon's rage. Tanka shuddered and revved, trying to resist, but his rusted red metal cracked and flaked, his engine spluttering, sending out oil and smoke. Cosmo held on, his power streaming through him, angry at the destruction the alien had caused.

Tanka's body was giving way, crumbling to pieces. In a burst of energy

the invader exploded, the force hurling Cosmo to the ground.

"You did it, Cosmo!" he heard. "You won! The Hub's DNA store is saved."

Cosmo staggered to his feet amidst the smoke and saw Nuri rushing to his side. Her spacesuit was torn and filthy but she was smiling broadly. She helped him up and gave him a hug. "You did it, Cosmo!"

"*We* did it," Cosmo replied. "Those gravity grenades of yours saved us."

Brain-E scuttled over. "Well done, Master Cosmo," the brainbot said.

"And you too, Brain-E," Cosmo replied. "I would never have thought of trying to get inside the alien if it hadn't been for you." He reached his hand down and the brainbot clung to his wrist, flashing its lights happily.

"Come on, let's get back to the Dragster," Brain-E said, "and tell G1 the good news."

***

Far beyond the galaxy in the Wrecking
Zone, the five-headed outlaw Kaos stared
aghast at a bank of digital monitors in
the cockpit of the battleship *Oblivion*.

"I-I-I don't believe it – Tanka's
exploded!" his fifth head yelled.

"He's been defeated!" the first head cried.

"But he was the last of our invaders!"
the second added.

"None have succeeded! Utterly
useless!" the third spat.

Kaos rewound the images on one of the
monitors, and a grainy picture of Cosmo
appeared with the power sword. "Five
metallicons all beaten by one wretched
Earthling boy!" his fifth head hissed. "How
are we ever to take control of the galaxy
while he is G-Watch's Agent Supreme?"

All five heads racked their brains.
"There must be a way to stop him. He
must have a weakness . . ."

Wugrat peered out from behind a monitor and squeaked. "Eeek!"

All five heads stared at it. "What's that you say, Wugrat?"

The purple rat twitched its whiskers. "Eeek!" it repeated, scratching the corner of a touch screen displaying a map of the galaxy. The screen zoomed in on a small blue-and-green planet spinning in space.

"Of course!" Kaos said, five sly grins spreading across his five faces. "Planet Earth . . ."

CHAPTER TEN

GALACTIC VACATION

The G-Watch team hitched a lift back to the pyramid portal in a ranger's buggy and took a final journey between dimensions to the landing area on the surface of Planet Kefu. The day was wearing on, and the light was now fading from the sky. Feeling exhausted but happy, they boarded the Dragster, and Nuri put in the call to G-Watch headquarters.

G1's face appeared on the ship's monitor,

grave with worry. "Well?" he asked.

"Relax, Chief," Nuri laughed. "Cosmo did it. He beat Tanka!"

G1 smiled with relief. "Well done, all of you," he said. "You have successfully completed your second mission. All five metallicons of the Wrecking Zone have been defeated – this invasion is over!"

Cosmo felt proud, but there was something still bothering him. "What about Kaos?" he asked G1. "Do you think that's it now? Do you think he'll leave the galaxy in peace?"

G1 frowned. "Kaos will never stop trying to defeat G-Watch and all that it stands for. His hatred for the free galaxy runs deep."

Cosmo didn't feel fear at G1's words. Indeed, a brave energy pulsed through him. "If Kaos returns, then I'll be ready for him," he said defiantly.

G1 smiled. "You are a worthy Agent

Supreme, Cosmo," he said. "Your father would be proud of you."

"So where to next?" Cosmo asked. "Back to G-Watch headquarters?"

G1's silver eyes twinkled. "Even Agent Supremes need to rest sometimes," he said with a smile. "I think you could do with a holiday, Cosmo. You may choose anywhere in the galaxy, courtesy of G-Watch."

"Woo-hoo!" Cosmo said, excited by the

115

idea of a galactic vacation. He thought for a moment of all the amazing planets he'd visited since he'd joined G-Watch, wondering where he'd really like to go next. Then he thought of his mum and his friends back on Earth. He smiled as he made his decision. "I think I'd like to return home for a while," he said. He glanced at Nuri. "Can Agent Nuri come too?"

"And me!" Brain-E added.

"A very wise choice," G1 said. "Of course you can all go. Have fun, team. You deserve it."

"Thanks, G1," the three friends replied.

The screen flickered and went blank as G1 signed off.

Cosmo turned to Nuri and grinned. "I'll take you for ice cream when we get there. You'll love it!"

Nuri laughed. "You're on, Cosmo! Maybe we can have another one of those Buzz Bars too . . ."

Cosmo flicked the switch to spaceship's thrusters and pull throttle, lifting the Dragster 7(the sky, then blasting off to the "Planet Earth, here we come!"

Have you collected the
ALIEN INVADERS gaming cards?

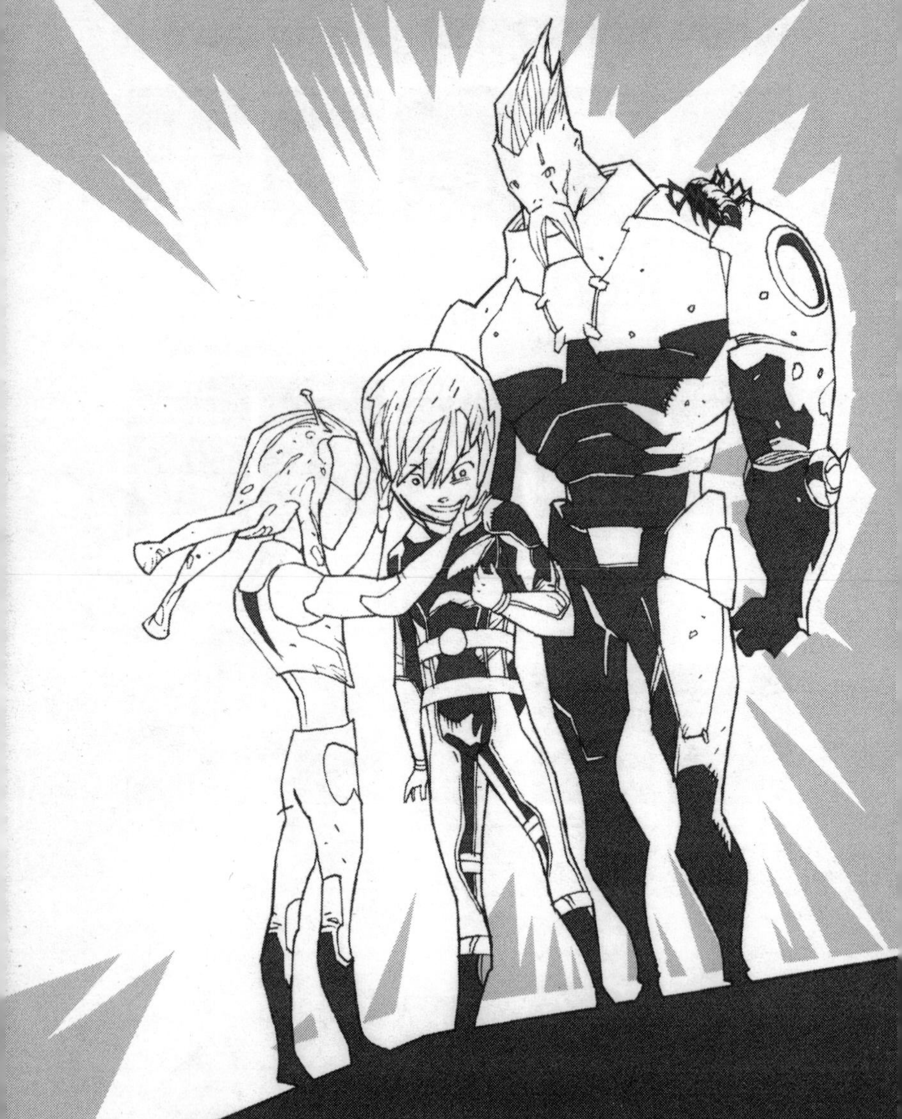

Supreme, Cosmo," he said. "Your father would be proud of you."

"So where to next?" Cosmo asked. "Back to G-Watch headquarters?"

G1's silver eyes twinkled. "Even Agent Supremes need to rest sometimes," he said with a smile. "I think you could do with a holiday, Cosmo. You may choose anywhere in the galaxy, courtesy of G-Watch."

"Woo-hoo!" Cosmo said, excited by the

idea of a galactic vacation. He thought for a moment of all the amazing planets he'd visited since he'd joined G-Watch, wondering where he'd really like to go next. Then he thought of his mum and his friends back on Earth. He smiled as he made his decision. "I think I'd like to return home for a while," he said. He glanced at Nuri. "Can Agent Nuri come too?"

"And me!" Brain-E added.

"A very wise choice," G1 said. "Of course you can all go. Have fun, team. You deserve it."

"Thanks, G1," the three friends replied.

The screen flickered and went blank as G1 signed off.

Cosmo turned to Nuri and grinned. "I'll take you for ice cream when we get there. You'll love it!"

Nuri laughed. "You're on, Cosmo! Maybe we can have another one of those Buzz Bars too . . ."

Cosmo flicked the switch to ignite the spaceship's thrusters and pulled back the throttle, lifting the Dragster 7000 up into the sky, then blasting off to the stars. "Planet Earth, here we come!"

NOW IT'S YOUR TURN

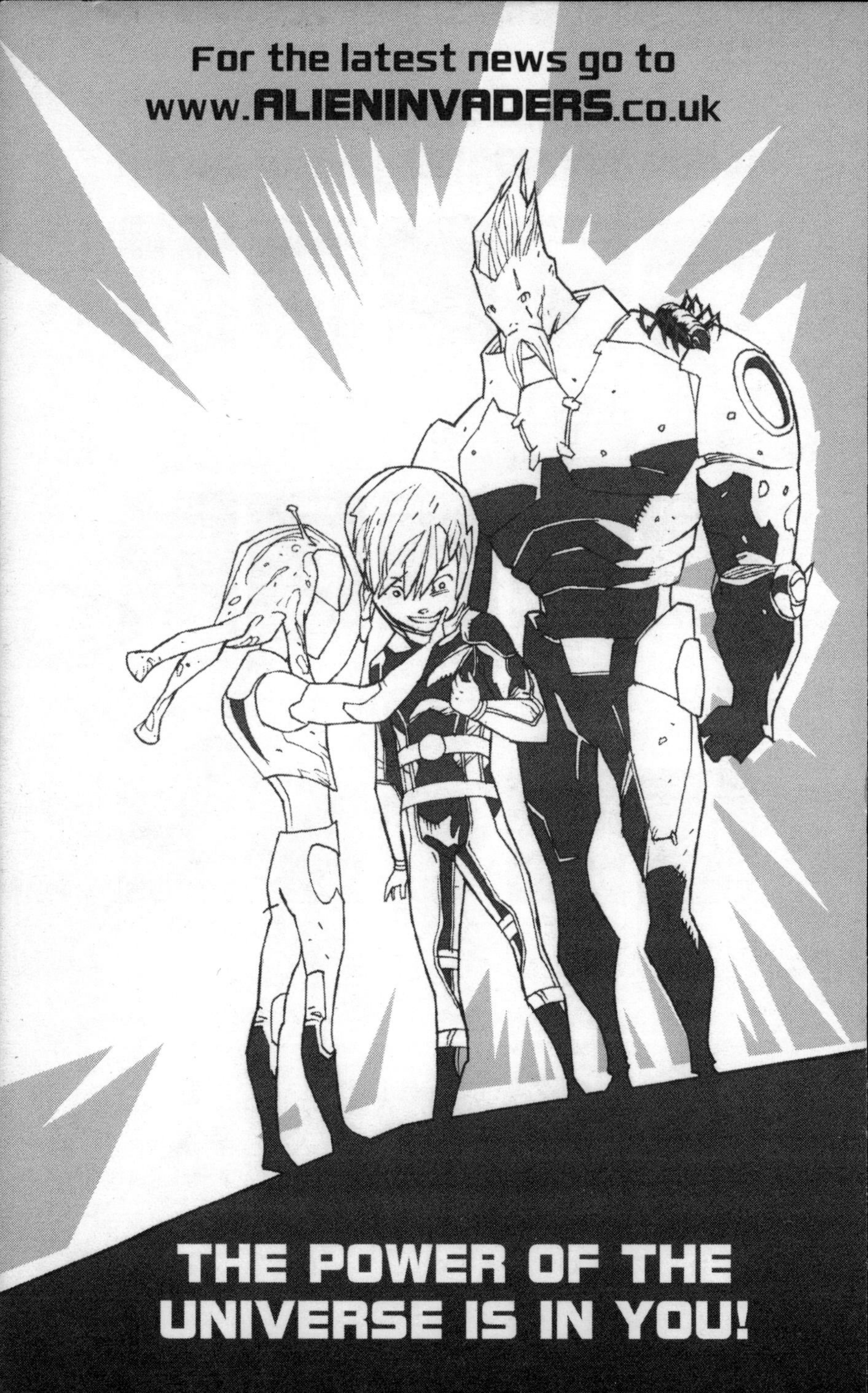
For the latest news go to
www.ALIENINVADERS.co.uk
THE POWER OF THE
UNIVERSE IS IN YOU!

Have you collected the
ALIEN INVADERS gaming cards?